This book is dedicated to all my children.
This story was created for you and now we can
share it with the rest of the world.

Peter Andre

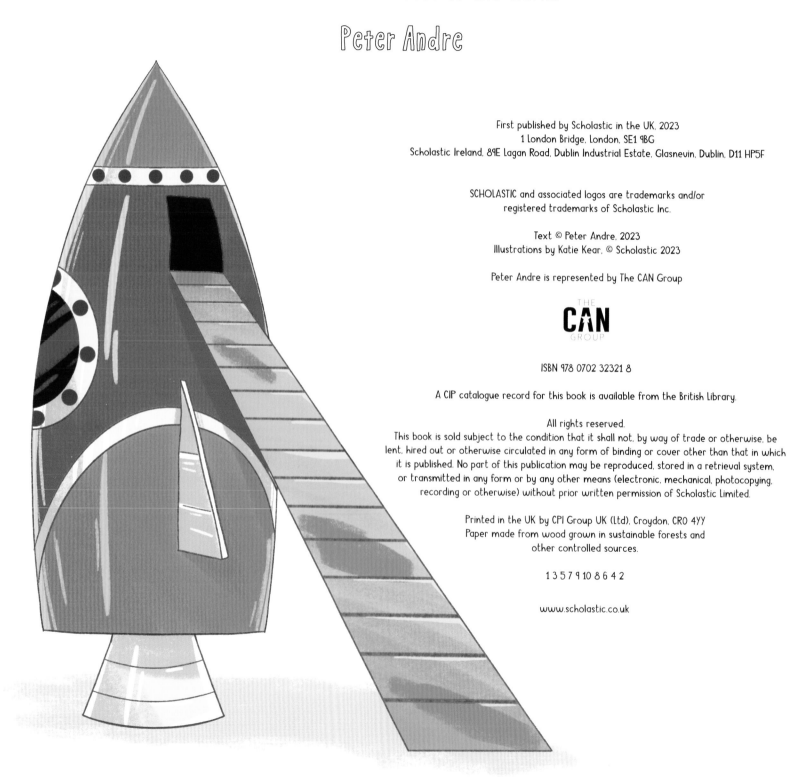

First published by Scholastic in the UK, 2023
1 London Bridge, London, SE1 9BG
Scholastic Ireland, 89E Lagan Road, Dublin Industrial Estate, Glasnevin, Dublin, D11 HP5F

Text © Peter Andre, 2023
Illustrations by Katie Kear, © Scholastic 2023

Peter Andre is represented by The CAN Group

THE
CAN
GROUP

ISBN 978 0702 32321 8

A CIP catalogue record for this book is available from the British Library.

Printed in the UK by CPI Group UK (ltd), Croydon, CR0 4YY
Paper made from wood grown in sustainable forests and
other controlled sources.

1 3 5 7 9 10 8 6 4 2

www.scholastic.co.uk

SUPER SPACE KIDS!
SAVE PLANET DRIZZLEBOTTOM

WRITTEN BY
PETER ANDRE

ILLUSTRATED BY
KATIE KEAR

CHAPTER ONE:
A BIG ANNOUNCEMENT

When Millie and her little brother Theo got to school on Monday morning, their scruffy teacher, Mr Walton, had some **amazing** news to share.

Our school has been chosen to fly to Planet Drizzlebottom on an *outer-space expedition!* The planet is totally grey and the Greylings have no idea why.

Millie's jaw dropped to the floor. She had always dreamed of travelling to other planets, but never ever thought her dream would come true.

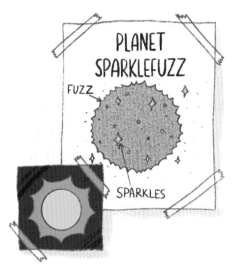

PLANET SPARKLEFUZZ

FUZZ

SPARKLES

Of course, she'd always imagined visiting places like **Planet Sparklefuzz** or the **Rainbow River Galaxy**... Not Planet Drizzlebottom, the dullest and dreariest sounding planet in the solar system.

Back at home that evening,
Millie's curiosity was building.

Did Greylings brush their teeth?

What kind of **food** did they **eat?**

Did they have pets?

And the most important question...

Why is the **planet** so totally **grey?**

She packed a notebook and her favourite pens and pencils, so she could write down everything she saw. What if she could discover something about Planet Drizzlebottom that nobody else could? What if *she* could be the person to solve the planet's problem?

Theo was equally *excited*. He couldn't wait to fly into space like a **real-life superhero** ... and he was looking forward to a few days off school!

CHAPTER TWO

READY FOR LIFT-OFF!

When the day of the launch finally arrived, Millie was raring to go.

Theo, wake up!

Theo rolled over and grunted, but there was no time to be tired.
The *most exciting* day of their lives was here!

The press had gathered by the launchpad. Every single TV channel was on standby with all the presidents and prime ministers of the world watching on. Prime Minister Gobblestop stepped up to the microphone.

Children of Nisbet Primary School – may you succeed on your expedition!

As the children boarded the spaceship, the humongous crowd erupted with cheers and claps and whistles. Millie turned to look at her mum and dad. She smiled in a way that said, "I'm going to do something special, just you watch."

Theo sat next to Millie and held her hand tight as they waited for the countdown. The engines began to ROAR.

10, 9, 8, 7, 6, 5, 4, 3, 2, 1

and LIFT-OFF!

CHAPTER THREE:
PLANET AHOY!

For three days and three nights they travelled through the cosmos, watching beautiful *shining stars* and *supernovas* glow **brighter** and **brighter**.
It was pure magic!

For Theo, time passed slowly.

Are we there yet?

asked Theo.

When the doors finally opened, Millie saw right away why everyone said Planet Drizzlebottom was SO grey. "They weren't kidding," she thought.

The **grass** was grey,

the **buildings** were grey,

the **aliens** were grey,

their **pets** were grey.

Everything was grey
- even the WEATHER!

"Surely there must be **colour** here somewhere," thought Millie. This must be the problem the planet needed help with!

"I'm going to find out!"

CHAPTER FOUR:
GRAND GREY TOUR

The next morning at their grey hotel, Millie and Theo brushed their teeth with grey toothpaste. In the mirror, Millie noticed that she and Theo were just as **colourful** as on Earth. Everywhere they walked, the floor lit up in vibrant colours, but would quickly fade back to grey as soon as they moved from their spot.

Millie was determined to figure out what was going on.

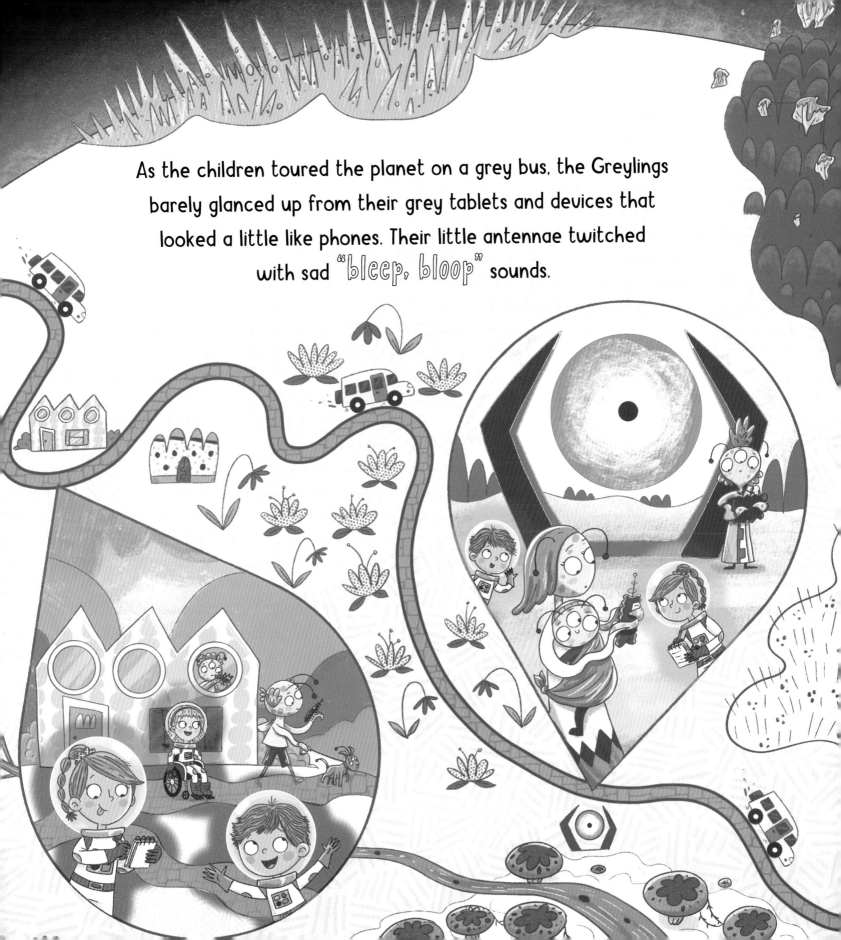

As the children toured the planet on a grey bus, the Greylings barely glanced up from their grey tablets and devices that looked a little like phones. Their little antennae twitched with sad "bleep, bloop" sounds.

Millie's class tried to work out how to help the Greylings.
Maybe the food was turning the planet grey?

But although the grey food didn't look very yummy,
it tasted surprisingly good. There was...

crowl

(which tasted a bit like apple)

streg

(which tasted a bit like peach,
and gave them bundles of energy)

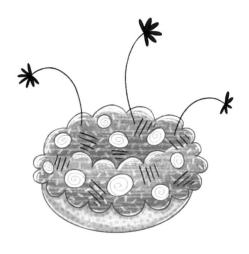

crumtuts

(delicious doughnut-like treats)

brub

(similar to Earth's chocolate
but, of course, grey)

The children took samples from the rocks, the rivers
and the atmosphere, but Millie was still curious what
was making the planet so grey.

CHAPTER FIVE:
A COLOURFUL SURPRISE

Their last day arrived, and Millie was disappointed that she hadn't worked out the problem.

Behind their hotel, she noticed a young Greyling playing with a little dog-like creature.

Suddenly, she realized something...

She grabbed Theo's hand and ran outside.

Look, Millie!

The alien and his pet were *bright* and **colourful!**

He smells like coconut!

Millie tried to talk to the Greyling. She wanted to ask how he was so colourful, but of course, she didn't speak the same language.

Even after they had joined their class on the bus to the launchpad, Millie could not stop thinking about the young alien and his pet. Why were they *colourful*, when everyone else was *grey*?

There had to be a simple reason!

Unless...

I've got it! I know why the planet is grey! Stop the bus!

Millie and Theo jumped out. Mr Walton and all the other children followed behind.

CHAPTER SIX:
MISSION SUCCESS!

"**Look around,**" said Millie.

"Look at what everybody is doing."

Everyone looked. Nearby, an alien wearing a big hat was scrolling on his device, looking bored. Another Greyling sitting on a bench was watching something on a device that looked like a tablet, her grey fluffy pet tied up at her feet.

Watch this!

As the pet grabbed the ball,
its fur turned shiny and bright.
Their owner dropped her tablet
and stood up in amazement.
Millie handed her the ball.

Lutch, Bubu!

This meant "catch, Bubu!"
in Drizzlebottom talk.

As the pet ran to catch the ball, its
owner began to smile. Just like that,
her antennae turned bright blue and
her tentacles started to shimmer.

Theo, Millie and the other children ran to help as many other Greylings as they could. As the aliens started to put their devices down, talk to each other and play with their pets, slowly but surely, everything around them turned into **full vibrant colour**.

The planet was **magically** changing, bit **by** bit.

The sky became **a sparkly blue**, unlike anything the children had ever seen.

The food turned all the colours of the rainbow, and looked far more **appetizing!**

Even the toothpaste transformed into bright, shimmering swirls.

Millie had done it!

CHAPTER SEVEN:
THE HEROES HEAD HOME

News travelled fast. The president of Drizzlebottom arrived to meet Millie and Theo. They were presented with what looked like **a key** to the planet! Although Millie and Theo couldn't understand the words spoken, they guessed that they were being thanked by the president.

Now it was time to go home.

From that day on, Millie and Theo were known as **Earth's true superheroes**. In fact, less than a week after they got home, the phone rang...

It seemed their adventures had only just begun!